GLUB!

For my precious Eleanor and Ollie with all my love x PL
For mum, love always, your dark haired bundle. x - SM

First published 2007
Evans Brothers Limited
2A Portman Mansions
Chiltern Street
London W1U 6NR

British Library Cataloguing in Publication Data

Little, Penny
   Glub! - (Spirals)
   1. Children's stories
   I. Title
   823.9'2 [J]

ISBN-13: 9780237534622 (HB)
ISBN-13: 9780237534615 (PB)

Printed in China

Series Editor: Nick Turpin
Design: Robert Walster
Production: Jenny Mulvanny

GLUB!

Penny Little
and Sue Mason

Evans

It was Jim's turn to clean out the goldfish bowl.

'Lucky will be quite safe in the kitchen sink,' said Dad, 'just don't forget to put in the plug!'

Lucky didn't much like being in the sink.

He looked at Jim fishily.

'Don't worry,' said Jim, 'your bowl will be sparkling clean soon.'

'Glub,' glubbed Lucky.

Jim was drying the
clean bowl when Dad
went to get a drink
of water.

He gulped it down, rinsed his mug,
and pulled out the plug.

The water swirled and gurgled
and disappeared …

'AAAGH!'
Jim stared into the empty sink.
'Where's Lucky?'

Dad skidded into the kitchen.
'OH NO,' he groaned.
'That was my fault ...
he's gone down the plug hole!'

Two big tears plopped
onto Jim's t-shirt.

'*Don't worry,*' announced Dad in his
best superhero voice, '*we'll find him!*'

Trapped in the slippery pipe,
Lucky flipped and flapped
and fluttered but he couldn't
get out …

Dad went to the garage to get his
tools and Jim peered down the plug
hole, but it was too dark to see
anything. 'Whatever you do, don't
turn on the tap,' called Dad from
the garage, 'he'll disappear in the
plumbing and ...'

OOOPS! TOO LATE!

Jim had already done it.

A swoosh of water scooped Lucky up and catapulted him down the pipe …

Whoooooooosh !

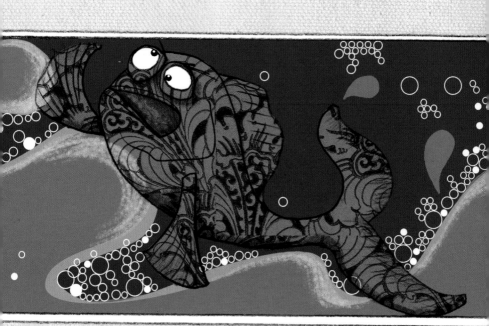

Dad scrambled under the sink with his torch. 'Let's hope that little fish is still in here,' he said to himself as he unscrewed the pipe.

Out flew an old earring, a baby tooth Jim thought he'd swallowed, a clumpy lump of disgusting hairy stuff, and an awful lot of water

...but no fish.

Meanwhile, Lucky was on an underwater roller coaster ride spinning and twisting ... twirling and swirling. He crossed his fins, closed his eyes and held his breath.

The rescue mission was not going
well at all but Dad refused to give up …
'Pass the hammer and the plunger,'
he shouted to Jim, 'I will find this fish.'

It was dark and creepy deep in the
pipes as the water swooshed him along.
    Lucky brushed past something
and a shiver of fear prickled down
his fish-bone.
    He swam away, his heart
thumping in his gills.

By tea-time Dad
had almost put the
kitchen sink back
together, but there
was still no sign of
Lucky.

Jim sat on the
back doorstep
feeling very sad.

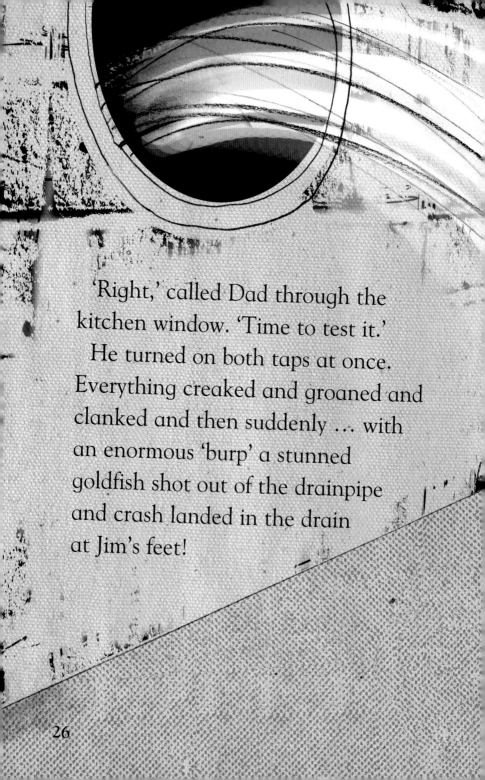

'Right,' called Dad through the
kitchen window. 'Time to test it.'
He turned on both taps at once.
Everything creaked and groaned and
clanked and then suddenly … with
an enormous 'burp' a stunned
goldfish shot out of the drainpipe
and crash landed in the drain
at Jim's feet!

'LUCKY!' yelled Jim, scooping him up
and popping him in his glass,
   'You're alive!'

Lucky goggled Jim in amazement.
'Glub!' he glubbed.

'Phew!' said Dad, 'that's a lucky
Lucky!'

And Jim, too thrilled to speak,
held the glass up to his face and
gave Lucky a gigantic glubby kiss!

Why not try reading a Spirals book?

Megan's Tick Tock Rocket by Andrew Fusek Peters,
Polly Peters, and Simona Dimitri
ISBN 978 0237 53342 7

Growl! by Vivian French and Tim Archbold
ISBN 978 0237 53345 8

John and the River Monster by Paul Harrison
and Ian Benfold Haywood
ISBN 978 0237 53344 1

Froggy Went a Hopping by Alan Durant and Sue Mason
ISBN 978 0237 53346 5

Glub! By Penny Little and Sue Mason
ISBN 978 0237 53461 5

Amy's Slippers by Mary Wilkinson and Simona Dimitri
ISBN 978 0237 53347 2

The Grumpy Queen by Valerie Wilding
and Simona Sanfilippo
ISBN 978 0237 53459 2

The Flamingo Who Forgot by Alan Durant
and Franco Rivolli
ISBN 978 0237 53343 4